4.⁵⁰

The Broken Soldier and the Maid of France

By
Henry van Dyke

Out of the beautiful myth that the soldiers of France have often been led and inspired on the battle-field by the vision of Joan of Arc, Dr. van Dyke has woven a tale of rare spiritual quality — of one poor Poilu who saw the Maid of France as in a dream and with her help went on gloriously with the fight he had been about to give up. A classic that will rank with "The Story of the Other Wise Man." It is illustrated with remarkable pictures by

F. E. Schoonover.

THE BROKEN SOLDIER
AND THE MAID
OF FRANCE

Books by

HENRY van DYKE

THE BROKEN SOLDIER
    AND THE MAID OF FRANCE
THE AMERICANISM OF WASHINGTON
THE CHRIST CHILD IN ART
THE LOST BOY
THE MANSION
THE STORY OF THE OTHER WISE MAN

———

HARPER & BROTHERS, NEW YORK
Established 1817

"God commands you," she cried. "It is for France"

The Broken Soldier and the Maid of France

By

HENRY VAN DYKE

With Illustrations by

FRANK E. SCHOONOVER

New York and London
Harper & Brothers Publishers
MCMXIX

Contents

		PAGE
The Meeting at the Spring	. . . . . .	3
The Green Confessional	. . . .	19
The Absolving Dream	. . . .	47
The Victorious Penance	. . . .	65

fellow of about thirty years, with dark
hair and eyes and a handsome, downcast face. His uniform was faded and
dusty; not a trace of the horizon-blue
was left; only a gray shadow. He had
no knapsack on his back, no gun on his
shoulder. Wearily and doggedly he plodded his way, without eyes for the veiled
beauty of the sleeping country. The
quick, firm military step was gone. He
trudged like a tramp, choosing always the
darker side of the road.

He was a figure of flight, a broken soldier.

Presently the road led him into a thick
forest of oaks and beeches, and so to the
crest of a hill overlooking a long, open
valley with wooded heights beyond. Below him was the pointed spire of some
temple or shrine, lying at the edge of the
wood, with no houses near it. Farther
down he could see a cluster of white houses
with the tower of a church in the center.
Other villages were dimly visible up and

fellow of about thirty years, with dark hair and eyes and a handsome, downcast face. His uniform was faded and dusty; not a trace of the horizon-blue was left; only a gray shadow. He had no knapsack on his back, no gun on his shoulder. Wearily and doggedly he plodded his way, without eyes for the veiled beauty of the sleeping country. The quick, firm military step was gone. He trudged like a tramp, choosing always the darker side of the road.

He was a figure of flight, a broken soldier.

Presently the road led him into a thick forest of oaks and beeches, and so to the crest of a hill overlooking a long, open valley with wooded heights beyond. Below him was the pointed spire of some temple or shrine, lying at the edge of the wood, with no houses near it. Farther down he could see a cluster of white houses with the tower of a church in the center. Other villages were dimly visible up and

THE BROKEN SOLDIER AND
THE MAID OF FRANCE

The Meeting at the Spring

ALONG the old Roman road that crosses the rolling hills from the upper waters of the Marne to the Meuse, a soldier of France was passing in the night.

In the broader pools of summer moonlight he showed as a hale and husky

The Meeting at
the Spring

Contents

PAGE

The Meeting at the Spring 3

The Green Confessional 19

The Absolving Dream 47

The Victorious Penance 65

down the valley on either slope. The cattle were lowing from the barnyards. The cocks crowed for the dawn. Already the moon had sunk behind the western trees. But the valley was still bathed in its misty, vanishing light. Over the eastern ridge the gray glimmer of the little day was rising, faintly tinged with rose. It was time for the broken soldier to seek his covert and rest till night returned.

So he stepped aside from the road and found a little dell thick with underwoods, and in it a clear spring gurgling among the ferns and mosses. Around the opening grew wild gooseberries and golden broom and a few tall spires of purple foxglove. He drew off his dusty boots and socks and bathed his feet in a small pool, drying them with fern leaves. Then he took a slice of bread and a piece of cheese from his pocket and made his breakfast. Going to the edge of the thicket, he parted the branches and peered out over the vale.

[5]

Its eaves sloped gently to the level floor where the river loitered in loops and curves. The sun was just topping the eastern hills; the heads of the trees were dark against a primrose sky.

In the fields the hay had been cut and gathered. The aftermath was already greening the moist places. Cattle and sheep sauntered out to pasture. A thin silvery mist floated here and there, spreading in broad sheets over the wet ground and shredding into filmy scarves and ribbons as the breeze caught it among the pollard willows and poplars on the border of the stream. Far away the water glittered where the river made a sudden bend or a long, smooth reach. It was like the flashing of distant shields. Overhead a few white clouds climbed up from the north. The rolling ridges, one after another, enfolded the valley as far as eye could see; pale green set in dark green, with here and there an arm of forest running down on a sharp promontory to meet and turn the meandering stream.

" It must be the valley of the Meuse," said the soldier. " My faith, but France is beautiful and tranquil here!"

The northerly wind was rising. The clouds climbed more swiftly. The poplars shimmered, the willows glistened, the veils of mist vanished. From very far away there came a rumbling thunder, heavy, insistent, continuous, punctuated with louder crashes.

" It is the guns," muttered the soldier, shivering. " It is the guns around Verdun! Those damned Boches!"

He turned back into the thicket and dropped among the ferns beside the spring. Stretching himself with a gesture of abandon, he pillowed his face on his crossed arms to sleep.

A rustling in the bushes roused him. He sprang to his feet quickly. It was a priest, clad in a dusty cassock, his long black beard streaked with gray. He came slowly treading up beside the trickling rivulet, carrying a bag on a stick over his shoulder.

"Good morning, my son," he said. "You have chosen a pleasant spot to rest."

The soldier, startled, but not forgetting his manners learned from boyhood, stood up and lifted his hand to take off his cap. It was already lying on the ground. "Good morning, Father," he answered. "I did not choose the place, but stumbled on it by chance. It is pleasant enough, for I am very tired and have need of sleep."

"No doubt," said the priest. "I can see that you look weary, and I beg you to pardon me if I have interrupted your repose. But why do you say you came here 'by chance'? If you are a good Christian you know that nothing is by chance. All is ordered and designed by Providence."

"So they told me in church long ago," said the soldier, coldly; "but now it does not seem so true—at least not with me."

[8]

The first feeling of friendliness and re-
spect into which he had been surprised was
passing. He had fallen back into the mood
of his journey—mistrust, secrecy, resent-
ment.

The priest caught the tone. His gray
eyes under their bushy brows looked kindly
but searchingly at the soldier and smiled
a little. He set down his bag and leaned
on his stick. " Well," he said, " I can
tell you one thing, my son. At all events,
it was not chance that brought me here.
I came with a purpose."

The soldier started, a little stung by
suspicion. " What then," he cried, roughly,
" were you looking for me? What do you
know of me? What is this talk of chance
and purpose?"

" Come, come," said the priest, his
smile spreading from his eyes to his lips,
" do not be angry. I assure you that I
know nothing of you whatever, not even
your name nor why you are here. When

[9]

I said that I came with a purpose I meant only that a certain thought, a wish, led me to this spot. Let us sit together awhile beside the spring and make better acquaintance."

"I do not desire it," said the soldier, with a frown.

"But you will not refuse it?" queried the priest, gently. "It is not good to refuse the request of one old enough to be your father. Look, I have here some excellent tobacco and cigarette-papers. Let us sit down and smoke together. I will tell you who I am and the purpose that brought me here."

The soldier yielded grudgingly, not knowing what else to do. They sat down on a mossy bank beside the spring, and while the blue smoke of their cigarettes went drifting under the little trees the priest began:

"My name is Antoine Courcy. I am the curé of Darney, a village among the Reaping Hook Hills, a few leagues south from here. For twenty-five years I have reaped the harvest of heaven in that blessed little field. I am sorry to leave it. But now this war, this great battle for freedom and the life of France, calls me. It is a divine vocation. France has need of all her sons to-day, even the old ones. I cannot keep the love of God in my heart unless I follow the love of country in my life. My younger brother, who used to be the priest of the next parish to mine, was in the army. He has fallen. I am going to replace him. I am on my way to join the troops—as a chaplain, if they will; if not, then as a private. I must get into the army of France or be left out of the host of heaven."

The soldier had turned his face away and was plucking the lobes from a frond of fern. "A brave resolve, Father," he said, with an ironic note. "But you have not yet told me what brings you off your road, to this place."

"I will tell you," replied the priest, eagerly; "it is the love of Jeanne d'Arc, the Maid who saved France long ago. You know about her?"

"A little," nodded the soldier. "I have learned in the school. She was a famous saint."

"Not yet a saint," said the priest, earnestly; "the Pope has not yet pronounced her a saint. But it will be done soon. Already he has declared her among the Blessed Ones. To me she is the most blessed of all. She never thought of herself or of a saint's crown. She gave her life entire for France. And this is the place that she came from! Think of that —right here!"

"I did not know that," said the soldier.

"But yes," the priest went on, kindling. "I tell you it was here that the Maid of France received her visions and set out to her work. You see that village below us —look out through the branches—that is

Domrémy, where she was born. That spire just at the edge of the wood—you saw that? It is the basilica they have built to her memory. It is full of pictures of her. It stands where the old beech-tree, ' Fair May,' used to grow. There she heard the voices and saw the saints who sent her on her mission. And this is the Gooseberry Spring, the Well of the Good Fairies. Here she came with the other children, at the festival of the well-dressing, to spread their garlands around it, and sing, and eat their supper on the green. Heavenly voices spoke to her, but the others did not hear them. Often did she drink of this water. It became a fountain of life springing up in her heart. I have come to drink at the same source. It will strengthen me as a sacrament. Come, son, let us take it together as we go to our duty in battle!"

Father Courcy stood up and opened his old black bag. He took out a small metal

[13]

cup. He filled it carefully at the spring. He made the sign of the cross over it.

"In the name of the Father, the Son, and the Holy Spirit," he murmured, "blessed and holy is this water." Then he held the cup toward the soldier. "Come, let us share it and make our vows together."

The bright drops trembled and fell from the bottom of the cup. The soldier sat still, his head in his hands.

"No," he answered, heavily, "I cannot take it. I am not worthy. Can a man take a sacrament without confessing his sins?"

Father Courcy looked at him with pitying eyes. "I see," he said, slowly; "I see, my son. You have a burden on your heart. Well, I will stay with you and try to lift it. But first I shall make my own vow."

He raised the cup toward the sky. A tiny brown wren sang canticles of rapture in the thicket. A great light came into the priest's face—a sun-ray from the east, far beyond the tree-tops.

"Blessed Jeanne d'Arc, I drink from thy fountain in thy name. I vow my life to thy cause. Aid me, aid this my son, to fight valiantly for freedom and for France. In the name of God, amen."

The soldier looked up at him. Wonder, admiration, and shame were struggling in the look. Father Courcy wiped the empty cup carefully and put it back in his bag. Then he sat down beside the soldier, laying a fatherly hand on his shoulder.

"Now, my son, you shall tell me what is on your heart."

The Green
Confessional

OR a long time the soldier remained silent. His head was bowed. His shoulders drooped. His hands trembled between his knees. He was wrestling with himself.

"No," he cried, at last, "I cannot, I dare not tell you. Unless, perhaps"—his voice faltered—"you could receive it under the seal of confession? But no. How could you do that? Here in the green woods? In the open air, beside a spring? Here is no confessional."

"Why not?" asked Father Courcy. "It is a good place, a holy place. Heaven is over our heads and very near. I will receive your confession here."

[19]

The soldier knelt among the flowers.
The priest pronounced the sacred words.
The soldier began his confession:

" I, Pierre Duval, a great sinner, confess
my fault, my most grievous fault, and pray
for pardon." He stopped for a moment
and then continued, " But first I must tell
you, Father, just who I am and where I
come from and what brings me here."

" Go on, Pierre Duval, go on. That is
what I am waiting to hear. Be simple and
very frank."

" Well, then, I am from the parish of
Laucourt, in the pleasant country of the
Barrois not far from Bar-sur-Aube. My
faith, but that is a pretty land, full of
orchards and berry-gardens! Our old
farm there is one of the prettiest and one
of the best, though it is small. It was
hard to leave it when the call to the colors
came, two years ago. But I was glad to
go. My heart was high and strong for
France. I was in the Nth Infantry. We

were in the center division under General Foch at the battle of the Marne. *Fichtre!* but that was fierce fighting! And what a general! He did not know how to spell 'defeat.' He wrote it 'victory.' Four times we went across that cursed Marsh of Saint-Gond. The dried mud was trampled full of dead bodies. The trickling streams of water ran red. Four times we were thrown back by the Boches. You would have thought that was enough. But the general did not think so. We went over again on the fifth day, and that time we stayed. The Germans could not stand against us. They broke and ran. The roads where we chased them were full of empty wine-bottles. In one village we caught three officers and a dozen men dead drunk. *Bigre!* what a fine joke!"

Pierre, leaning back upon his heels, was losing lines in his recital. His face lighted up, his hands were waving. Father Courcy bent forward with shining eyes.

" Continue," he cried. " This is a beautiful confession—no sin yet. Continue, Pierre."

" Well, then, after that we were fighting here and there, on the Aisne, on the Ailette, everywhere. Always the same story— Germans rolling down on us in flood, green-gray waves. But the foam on them was fire and steel. The shells of the barrage swept us like hailstones. We waited, waited in our trenches, till the green-gray mob was near enough. Then the word came. *Sapristi!* We let loose with mitrailleuse, rifle, field-gun, everything that would throw death. It did not seem like fighting with men. It was like trying to stop a monstrous thing, a huge, terrible mass that was rushing on to overwhelm us. The waves tumbled and broke before they reached us. Sometimes they fell flat. Sometimes they turned and rushed the other way. It was wild, wild, like a change of the wind and tide in a storm, everything

[22]

torn and confused. Then perhaps the word came to go over the top and at them. That was furious. That was fighting with men, for sure—bayonet, revolver, rifle-butt, knife, anything that would kill. Often I sickened at the blood and the horror of it. But something inside of me shouted: 'Fight on! It is for France. It is for *"L'Alouette,"* thy farm; for thy wife, thy little ones. Wilt thou let them be ruined by those beasts of Boches? What are they doing here on French soil? Brigands, butchers, Apaches! Drive them out; and if they will not go, kill them so they can do no more shameful deeds. Fight on!' So I killed all I could."

The priest nodded his head grimly. "You were right, Pierre; your voice spoke true. It was a dreadful duty that you were doing. The Gospel tells us, if we are smitten on one cheek we must turn the other. But it does not tell us to turn the cheek of a little child, of the woman we love, of the country we belong to. No! that would be disgraceful, wicked, un-Christian. It would be to betray the innocent! Continue, my son."

"Well, then," Pierre went on, his voice deepening and his face growing more tense, "then we were sent to Verdun. That was the hottest place of all. It was at the top of the big German drive. The whole sea rushed and fell on us—big guns, little guns, poison-gas, hand-grenades, liquid fire, bayonets, knives, and trench-clubs. Fort after fort went down. The whole pack of hell was loose and raging. I thought of that crazy, chinless Crown Prince sitting in his safe little cottage hidden in the woods somewhere—they say he had flowers and vines planted around it—drinking stolen champagne and sicking on his dogs of death. He was in no danger. I cursed him in my heart, that blood-lord! The shells rained on Verdun. The houses were riddled; the cathedral was pierced in a dozen places; a hundred fires broke out. The old citadel held good. The outer forts to the north and east were taken. Only the last ring was left. We common soldiers did not know much about what was happening. The big battle was beyond our horizon. But that General Pétain, he knew it all. Ah, that is a wise man, I can tell you! He sent us to this place or that place where the defense was most needed. We went gladly, without fear or holding back. We were resolute that those mad dogs should not get through. 'They shall not pass!' And they did not pass!"

"Glorious!" cried the priest, drinking the story in. "And you, Pierre? Where were you, what were you doing?"

"I was at Douaumont, that fort on the highest hill of all. The Germans took it. It cost them ten thousand men. The ground around it was like a wood-yard piled with logs. The big shell-holes were

[25]

full of corpses. There were a few of us
that got away. Then our company was
sent to hold the third redoubt on the slope
in front of Fort de Vaux. Perhaps you
have heard of that redoubt. That was a
bitter job. But we held it many days and
nights. The Boches pounded us from
Douaumont and from the village of Vaux.
They sent wave after wave up the slope
to drive us out. But we stuck to it. That
ravine of La Caillette was a boiling caldron
of men. It bubbled over with smoke and
fire. Once, when their second wave had
broken just in front of us, we went out to
hurry the fragments down the hill. Then
the guns from Douaumont and the village
of Vaux hammered us. Our men fell like
nine-pins. Our lieutenant called to us to
turn back. Just then a shell tore away
his right leg at the knee. It hung by the
skin and tendons. He was a brave lad.
I could not leave him to die there. So
I hoisted him on my back. Three shots

struck me. They felt just like hard blows from a heavy fist. One of them made my left arm powerless. I sank my teeth in the sleeve of my lieutenant's coat as it hung over my shoulder. I must not let him fall off my back. Somehow—God knows how—I gritted through to our redoubt. They took my lieutenant from my shoulders. And then the light went out."

The priest leaned forward, his hands stretched out around the soldier. "But you are a hero," he cried. "Let me embrace you!"

The soldier drew back, shaking his head sadly. "No," he said, his voice breaking —"no, my father, you must not embrace me now. I may have been a brave man once. But now I am a coward. Let me tell you everything. My wounds were bad, but not desperate. The *brancardiers* carried me down to Verdun, at night, I suppose, but I was unconscious; and so to the

[27]

hospital at Vaudelaincourt. There were days and nights of blankness mixed with pain. Then I came to my senses and had rest. It was wonderful. I thought that I had died and gone to heaven. Would God it had been so! Then I should have been with my lieutenant. They told me he had passed away in the redoubt. But that hospital was beautiful, so clean and quiet and friendly. Those white nurses were angels. They handled me like a baby. I would have liked to stay there. I had no desire to get better. But I did. One day several officers visited the hospital. They came to my cot, where I was sitting up. The highest of them brought out a Cross of War and pinned it on the breast of my nightshirt. 'There,' he said, 'you are decorated, Pierre Duval! You are one of the heroes of France. You are soon going to be perfectly well and to fight again bravely for your country.' I thanked him, but I knew better. My body might get perfectly well, but something in my soul was broken. It was worn out. The thin spring had snapped. I could never fight again. Any loud noise made me shake all over. I knew that I could never face a battle—impossible! I should certainly lose my nerve and run away. It is a damned feeling, that broken something inside of one. I can't describe it."

Pierre stopped for a moment and moistened his dry lips with the tip of his tongue.

"I know," said Father Courcy. "I understand perfectly what you want to say. It was like being lost and thinking that nothing could save you; a feeling that is piercing and dull at the same time, like a heavy weight pressing on you with sharp stabs in it. It was what they call shell-shock, a terrible thing. Sometimes it drives men crazy for a while. But the doctors know what to do for that malady. It passes. You got over it."

"No," answered Pierre, "the doctors

may not have known that I had it. At
all events, they did not know what to do
for it. It did not pass. It grew worse.
But I hid it, talking very little, never
telling anybody how I felt. They said I
was depressed and needed cheering up.
All the while there was that black snake
coiled around my heart, squeezing tighter
and tighter. But my body grew stronger
every day. The wounds were all healed.
I was walking around. In July the doctor-
in-chief sent for me to his office. He said:
' You are cured, Pierre Duval, but you
are not yet fit to fight. You are low in
your mind. You need cheering up. You
are to have a month's furlough and repose.
You shall go home to your farm. How is
it that you call it? ' I suppose I had been
babbling about it in my sleep and one of
the nurses had told him. He was always
that way, that little Doctor Roselly, taking
an interest in the men, talking with them
and acting friendly. I said the farm was

called '*L'Alouette*'—rather a foolish name.
'Not at all,' he answered; 'it is a fine
name, with the song of a bird in it. Well,
you are going back to "*L'Alouette*" to
hear the lark sing for a month, to kiss
your wife and your children, to pick gooseberries and currants. Eh, my boy, what
do you think of that? Then, when the
month is over, you will be a new man. You
will be ready to fight again at Verdun.
Remember they have not passed and they
shall not pass! Good luck to you, Pierre
Duval.' So I went back to the farm as
fast as I could go."

He was silent for a few moments, letting
his thoughts wander through the pleasant
paths of that little garden of repose. His
eyes were dreaming, his lips almost smiled.

"It was sweet at '*L'Alouette*,' very
sweet, Father. The farm was in pretty
good order and the kitchen-garden was all
right, though the flowers had been a little
neglected. You see, my wife, Joséphine,

[31]

she is a very clever woman. She had kept up the things that were the most necessary. She had hired one of the old neighbors and a couple of boys to help her with the plowing and planting. The harvest she sold as it stood. Our yoke of cream-colored oxen and the roan horse were in good condition. Little Pierrot, who is five, and little Josette, who is three, were as brown as berries. They hugged me almost to death. But it was Joséphine herself who was the best of all. She is only twenty-six, Father, and so beautiful still, with her long chestnut hair and her eyes like brown stones shining under the waters of a brook. I tell you it was good to get her in my arms again and feel her lips on mine. And to wake in the early morning, while the birds were singing, and see her face beside me on the white pillow, sleeping like a child, that was a little bit of Paradise. But I do wrong to tell you of all this, Father."

"Proceed, my big boy," nodded the

priest. "You are saying nothing wrong. I was a man before I was a priest. It is all natural, what you are saying, and all according to God's law—no sin in it. Proceed. Did your happiness do you good?"

Pierre shook his head doubtfully. The look of dejection came back to his face. He frowned as if something puzzled and hurt him. "Yes and no! That is the strange thing. It made me thankful—that goes without saying. But it did not make me any stronger in my heart. Perhaps it was too sweet. I thought too much of it. I could not bear to think of anything else. The idea of the war was hateful, horrible, disgusting. The noise and the dirt of it, the mud in the autumn and the bitter cold in the winter, the rats and the lice in the dugouts! And then the fury of the charge, and the everlasting killing, killing, or being killed! The danger had seemed little or nothing to me when I was there. But at a distance it was frightful, unendurable. I knew that I could never stand up to it again. Besides, already I had done my share—enough for two or three men. Why must I go back into that hell? It was not fair. Life was too dear to be risking it all the time. I could not endure it. France? France? Of course I love France. But my farm and my life with Joséphine and the children mean more to me. The thing that made me a good soldier is broken inside me. It is beyond mending."

His voice sank lower and lower. Father Courcy looked at him gravely.

"But your farm is a part of France. You belong to France. He that saveth his life shall lose it!"

"Yes, yes, I know. But my farm is such a small part of France. I am only one man. What difference does one man make, except to himself? Moreover, I had done my part, that was certain. Twenty times, really, my life had been lost. Why must I throw it away again? Listen, Father. There is a village in the Vosges, near the Swiss border, where a relative of mine lives. If I could get to him he would take me in and give me some other clothes and help me over the frontier into Switzerland. There I could change my name and find work until the war is over. That was my plan. So I set out on my journey, following the less-traveled roads, tramping by night and sleeping by day. Thus I came to this spring at the same time as you by chance, by pure chance. Do you see?"

Father Courcy looked very stern and seemed about to speak in anger. Then he shook his head, and said, quietly: "No, I do not see that at all. It remains to be seen whether it was by chance. But tell me more about your sin. Did you let your wife, Joséphine, know what you were going to do? Did you tell her good-by, parting for Switzerland?"

[35]

"Why, no! I did not dare. She would never have forgiven me. So I slipped down to the post-office at Bar-sur-Aube and stole a telegraph blank. It was ten days before my furlough was out. I wrote a message to myself calling me back to the colors at once. I showed it to her. Then I said good-by. I wept. She did not cry one tear. Her eyes were stars. She embraced me a dozen times. She lifted up each of the children to hug me. Then she cried: 'Go now, my brave man. Fight well. Drive the damned Boches out. It is for us and for France. God protect you. *Au revoir!*' I went down the road silent. I felt like a dog. But I could not help it."

"And you were a dog," said the priest, sternly. "That is what you were, and what you remain unless you can learn to help it. You lied to your wife. You forged; you tricked her who trusted you. You have done the thing which you yourself say she would never forgive. If she loves you and prays for you now, you have stolen that love and that prayer. You are a thief. A true daughter of France could never love a coward to-day."

"I know, I know," sobbed Pierre, burying his face in the weeds. "Yet I did it partly for her, and I could not do otherwise."

"Very little for her and a hundred times for yourself," said the priest, indignantly. "Be honest. If there was a little bit of love for her, it was the kind of love she did not want. She would spit upon it. If you are going to Switzerland now you are leaving her forever. You can never go back to Joséphine again. You are a deserter. She would cast you out, coward!"

The broken soldier lay very still, almost as if he were dead. Then he rose slowly to his feet, with a pale, set face. He put his hand behind his back and drew out a revolver. "It is true," he said, slowly,

[37]

" I am a coward. But not altogether such a coward as you think, Father. It is not merely death that I fear. I could face that, I think. Here, take this pistol and shoot me now! No one will know. You can say you shot a deserter, or that I attacked you. Shoot me now, Father, and let me out of this trouble."

Father Courcy looked at him with amazement. Then he took the pistol, uncocked it cautiously, and dropped it behind him. He turned to Pierre and regarded him curiously. " Go on with your confession, Pierre. Tell me about this strange kind of cowardice which can face death."

The soldier dropped on his knees again and went on, in a low, shaken voice: " It is this, Father. By my broken soul, this is the very root of it. *I am afraid of fear.*"

The priest thought for an instant. " But that is not reasonable, Pierre. It is nonsense. Fear cannot hurt you. If you fight it you can conquer it. At least you can disregard it, march through it, as if it were not there."

"Not this fear," argued the soldier, with a peasant's obstinacy. "This is something very big and dreadful. It has no shape, but a dead-white face and red, blazing eyes full of hate and scorn. I have seen it in the dark. It is stronger than I am. Since something is broken inside of me, I know I can never conquer it. No, it would wrap its shapeless arms around me and stab me to the heart with its fiery eyes. I should turn and run in the middle of the battle. I should trample on my wounded comrades. I should be shot in the back and die in disgrace. O my God! my God! who can save me from this? It is horrible. I cannot bear it."

The priest laid his hand gently on Pierre's quivering shoulder. "Courage, my son!"

"She would never speak to a man like me. She is a great saint, very high in heaven."

"She was a farmer's lass, a peasant like yourself. She would speak to you, gladly and kindly, if you saw her, and in your own language, too. Trust her."

"But I do not know enough about her."

"Listen, Pierre. I have thought for you. I will appoint the first part of your penance. You shall take the risk of being recognized and caught. You shall go down to that village there and visit the places that belong to her—her basilica, her house, her church. Then you shall come back here and wait until you know—until you surely know what you must do. Will you promise this?"

Pierre had risen and looked up at the priest with tear-stained face. But his eyes were quieter. "Yes, Father, I can promise you this much faithfully."

"Now I must go my way. Farewell, my son. Peace in war be with you." He held out his hand.

Pierre took it reverently. "And with you, Father," he murmured.

The Absolving
Dream

They also were pilgrims drawn by the love of
Jeanne d'Arc to Domrémy

NTOINE COURCY was one of those who are fitted and trained by nature for the cure of souls. If you had spoken to him of psychiatry he would not have understood you. The long word would have been Greek to him. But the thing itself he knew well. The preliminary penance which he laid upon Pierre Duval was remedial. It belonged to the true healing art, which works first in the spirit.

When the broken soldier went down the hill, in the blaze of the mid-morning sunlight, toward Domrémy, there was much misgiving and confusion in his thoughts. He did not comprehend why he was going, except that he had promised. He was not sure that some one might not know him, or perhaps out of mere curiosity stop him and question him. It was a reluctant journey.

Yet it was in effect an unconscious pilgrimage to the one health-resort that his soul needed. For Domrémy and the region round about are saturated with the most beautiful story of France. The life of Jeanne d'Arc, simple and mysterious, humble and glorious, most human and most heavenly, flows under that place like a hidden stream, rising at every turn in springs and fountains. The poor little village lives in and for her memory. Her presence haunts the ridges and the woods, treads the green pastures, follows the white road beside the river, and breathes in the never-resting valley-wind that marries the flowers in June and spreads their seed in August.

At the small basilica built to her memory on the place where her old beech-tree,

" Fair May," used to stand, there was an ancient caretaker who explained to Pierre the pictures from the life of the Maid with which the walls are decorated. They are stiff and conventional, but the old man found them wonderful and told with zest the story of *La Pucelle*—how she saw her first vision; how she recognized the Dauphin in his palace at Chinon; how she broke the siege of Orléans; how she saw Charles crowned in the cathedral at Rheims; how she was burned at the stake in Rouen. But they could not kill her soul. She saved France.

In the village church there was a priest from the border of Alsace, also a pilgrim like Pierre, but one who knew the shrine better. He showed the difference between the new and the old parts of the building. Certain things the Maid herself had seen and touched.

" Here is the old holy-water basin, an antique, broken column hollowed out on top. Here her fingers must have rested often. Before this ancient statue of St. Michel she must have often knelt to say her prayers. The curé of the parish was a friend of hers and loved to talk with her. She was a good girl, devout and obedient, not learned, but a holy and great soul. She saved France."

In the house where she was born, and passed her childhood, a crippled old woman was custodian. It was a humble dwelling of plastered stone standing between two tall fir-trees, with ivy growing over the walls, lilies and hollyhocks blooming in the garden. Pierre found it not half so good a house as *"L'Alouette."* But to the custodian it was more precious than a palace. In this upper room with its low mullioned window the Maid began her life. Here, in the larger room below, is the kneeling statue which the Princess Marie d'Orléans made of her. Here, to the right, under the sloping roof, with its worm-eaten beams, she slept and prayed and worked.

"See, here is the bread-board between two timbers where she cut the bread for the *croûte-au-pot*. From this small window she looked at night and saw the sanctuary light burning in the church. Here, also, as well as in the garden and in the woods, her heavenly voices spoke to her and told her what she must do for her king and her country. She was not afraid or ashamed, though she lived in so small a house. Here in this very room she braided her hair and put on her red dress, and set forth on foot for her visit to Robert de Baudricourt at Vaucouleurs. He was a rough man and at first he received her roughly. But at last she convinced him. He gave her a horse and arms and sent her to the king. She saved France."

At the rustic inn Pierre ate thick slices of dark bread and drank a stoup of thin red wine at noon. He sat at a bare table

[51]

livered Orléans. Why not credit her when she says she heard God and the saints speaking to her? The proof of it was in what she did. Have you read the story of her trial? How clear and steady her answers were! The judges could not shake her. Yet at any moment she could have saved her life by denying the voices. It was because she knew, because she was sure, that she could not deny. Her vision was a part of her real life. She was the mother of French patriotism—yes. But she was also the daughter of true faith. That was her power."

"Well," said the younger man, "she sacrificed herself and she saved France. That was the great thing."

"Yes," said the elder man, stretching his hand across the table to clasp the hand of his companion, "there is nothing greater than that. If we do that, God will forgive us all."

They put on their caps to go. Pierre

rose and stood at attention. They returned his salute with a friendly smile and passed out.

After a few moments he finished his bread and wine, paid his score, and followed them. He watched them going down the village street toward the railway station. Then he turned and walked slowly back to the spring in the dell.

The afternoon was hot, in spite of the steady breeze which came out of the north. The air felt as if it had passed through a furnace. The low, continuous thunder of the guns rolled up from Verdun, with now and then a sharper clap from St. Mihiel.

Pierre was very tired. His head was heavy, his heart troubled. He lay down among the ferns, looking idly at the foxglove spires above him and turning over in his mind the things he had heard and seen at Domrémy. Presently he fell into a profound sleep.

How long it was he could not tell, but

suddenly he became aware of some one near him. He sprang up. A girl was standing beside the spring.

She wore a bright-red dress and her feet were bare. Her black hair hung down her back. Her eyes were the color of a topaz. Her form was tall and straight. She carried a distaff under her arm and looked as if she had just come from following the sheep.

"Good day, shepherdess," said Pierre. Then a strange thought struck him, and he fell on his knees. "Pardon, lady," he stammered. "Forgive my rudeness. You are of the high society of heaven, a saint. You are called Jeanne d'Arc?"

She nodded and smiled. "That is my name," said she. "Sometimes they call me *La Pucelle*, or the Maid of France. But you were right, I am a shepherdess, too. I have kept my father's sheep in the fields down there, and spun from the distaff while I watched them. I knew

[56]

how to sew and spin as well as any girl in the Barrois or Lorraine. Will you not stand up and talk with me?"

Pierre rose, still abashed and confused. He did not quite understand how to take this strange experience—too simple for a heavenly apparition, too real for a common dream. "Well, then," said he, "if you are a shepherdess why are you here? There are no sheep here."

"But yes. You are one of mine. I have come here to seek you."

"Do you know me, then? How can I be one of yours?"

"Because you are a soldier of France and you are in trouble."

Pierre's head drooped. "A broken soldier," he muttered, "not fit to speak to you. I am running away because I am afraid of fear."

She threw back her head and laughed. "You speak very bad French. There is no such thing as being afraid of fear. For if you are afraid of it, you hate it. If you hate it, you will have nothing to do with it. And if you have nothing to do with it, it cannot touch you; it is nothing."

"But for you, a saint, it is easy to say that. You had no fear when you fought. You knew you would not be killed."

"I was no more sure of that than the other soldiers. Besides, when they bound me to the stake at Rouen and kindled the fire around me I knew very well that I should be killed. But there was no fear in it. Only peace."

"Ah, you were strong, a warrior born. You were not wounded and broken."

"Four times I was wounded," she answered, gravely. "At Orléans a bolt went through my right shoulder. At Paris a lance tore my thigh. I never saw the blood of Frenchmen flow without feeling my heart stand still. I was not a warrior born. I knew not how to ride or fight. But I did it. What we must needs do that we can do. Soldier, do not look on the ground. Look up."

Then a strange thing took place before his eyes. A wondrous radiance, a mist of light, enveloped and hid the shepherdess. When it melted she was clad in shining armor, sitting on a white horse, and lifting a bare sword in her left hand.

"God commands you," she cried. "It is for France. Be of good cheer. Do not retreat. The fort will soon be yours!"

How should Pierre know that this was the cry with which the Maid had rallied her broken men at Orléans when the fort of *Les Tourelles* fell? What he did know was that something seemed to spring up within him to answer that call. He felt that he would rather die than desert such a leader.

The figure on the horse turned away as if to go.

"Do not leave me," he cried, stretching out his hands to her. "Stay with me. I will obey you joyfully."

[59]

She turned again and looked at him very earnestly. Her eyes shone deep into his heart. "Here I cannot stay," answered a low, sweet, womanly voice. "It is late, and my other children need me."

"But forgiveness? Can you give that to me—a coward?"

"You are no coward. Your only fault was to doubt a brave man."

"And my wife? May I go back and tell her?"

"No, surely. Would you make her hear slander of the man she loves? Be what she believes you and she will be satisfied."

"And the absolution, the word of peace? Will you speak that to me?"

Her eyes shone more clearly; the voice sounded sweeter and steadier than ever. "After the penance comes the absolution. You will find peace only at the lance's point. Son of France, go, go, go! I will help you. Go hardily to Verdun."

Pierre sprang forward after the receding

figure, tried to clasp the knee, the foot of the Maid. As he fell to the ground something sharp pierced his hand. It must be her spur, thought he.

Then he was aware that his eyes were shut. He opened them and looked at his hand carefully. There was only a scratch on it, and a tiny drop of blood. He had torn it on the thorns of the wild-gooseberry bushes.

His head lay close to the clear pool of the spring. He buried his face in it and drank deep. Then he sprang up, shaking the drops from his mustache, found his cap and pistol, and hurried up the glen toward the old Roman road.

"No more of that damned foolishness about Switzerland," he said, aloud. "I belong to France. I am going with the other boys to save her. I was born for that." He took off his cap and stood still for a moment. He spoke as if he were taking an oath. "By Jeanne d'Arc!"

The Victorious
Penance

The Victorious Penance

IT never occurred to Pierre Duval, as he trudged those long kilometers toward the front, that he was doing a penance.

The joy of a mind made up is a potent cordial.

The greetings of comrades on the road put gladness into his heart and strength into his legs.

It was a hot and dusty journey, and a sober one. But it was not a sad one. He was going toward that for which he was born. He was doing that which France asked of him, that which God told him to do. Joséphine would be glad and proud of him. He would never be ashamed to meet her eyes. As he went, alone or in company with others, he whistled and sang a bit. He thought of "*L'Alouette*" a good deal. But not too much. He thought also of the forts of Douaumont and Vaux.

"*Dame!*" he cried to himself. "If I could help to win them back again! That would be fine! How sick that would make those cursed Boches and their knock-kneed Crown Prince!"

At the little village of the headquarters behind Verdun he found many old friends and companions. They greeted him with cheerful irony.

"Behold the prodigal! You took your time about coming back, didn't you? Was the hospital to your taste, the nurses pretty? How is the wife? Any more children? How goes it, old man?"

"No more children yet," he answered, grinning; "but all goes well. I have come back from a far country, but I find the pigs are still grunting. What have you done to our old cook?"

"Nothing at all," was the joyous reply. "He tried to swim in his own soup and he was drowned."

When Pierre reported to the officer of the day, that busy functionary consulted the record.

"You are a day ahead of your time, Pierre Duval," he said, frowning slightly.

"Yes, sir," answered the soldier. "It costs less to be a day ahead than a day too late."

"That is well," said the officer, smiling in his red beard. "You will report to-morrow to your regiment at the citadel. You have a new colonel, but the regiment is busy in the old way."

As Pierre saluted and turned to go out his eye caught the look of a general officer who stood near, watching. He was a square, alert, vigorous man, his face bronzed by the suns of many African campaigns, his eyes full of intelligence, humor, and courage. It was Guillaumat, the new commander of the Army of Verdun.

"You are prompt, my son," said he, pleasantly, "but you must remember not to be in a hurry. You have been in hospital. Are you well again? Nothing broken?"

"Something was broken, my General," responded the soldier, gravely, "but it is mended."

"Good!" said the general. "Now for the front, to beat the Germans at their own game. *We shall get them.* It may be long, but we shall get them!"

That was the autumn of the offensive of 1916, by which the French retook, in ten days, what it had cost the Germans many months to gain.

Pierre was there in that glorious charge in the end of October which carried the heights of Douaumont and took six thousand prisoners. He was there at the recapture of the Fort de Vaux which the Germans evacuated in the first week of November. In the last rush up the slope, where he had fought long ago, a stray shell, an inscrutable messenger of fate, coming from far away, no one knows whence, caught him and ripped him horribly across the body.

It was a desperate mass of wounds. But the men of his squad loved their corporal. He still breathed. They saw to it that he was carried back to the little transit hospital just behind the Fort de Souville.

It was a rude hut of logs, covered with sand-bags, on the slope of the hill. The ruined woods around it were still falling to the crash of far-thrown shells. In the close, dim shelter of the inner room Pierre came to himself.

He looked up into the face of Father Courcy. A light of recognition and gratitude flickered in his eyes. It was like finding an old friend in the dark.

"Welcome!—But the fort?" he gasped.

"It is ours," said the priest.

Something like a smile passed over the face of Pierre. He could not speak for a long time. The blood in his throat choked him. At last he whispered:

"Tell Joséphine—love."

Father Courcy bowed his head and took Pierre's hand. "Surely," he said. "But now, my dear son Pierre, I must prepare you—"

The struggling voice from the cot broke in, whispering slowly, with long intervals: "Not necessary. . . . I know already. . . . The penance. . . . France. . . . Jeanne d'Arc. . . . It is done."

A few drops of blood gushed from the corner of his mouth. The look of peace that often comes to those who die of gunshot wounds settled on his face. His eyes grew still as the priest laid the sacred wafer on his lips. The broken soldier was made whole.

THE END